# The Tale of

# Peeky Peeper

## by Lorraine Holnback Brodek

A CHRISTMAS STORY GAME

tate publishing
CHILDREN'S DIVISION

Published by Tate Publishing & Enterprises, LLC
127 E. Trade Center Terrace | Mustang, Oklahoma 73064 USA
1.888.361.9473 | www.tatepublishing.com

Tate Publishing is committed to excellence in the publishing industry. The company reflects the philosophy established by the founders, based on Psalm 68:11,
*"The Lord gave the word and great was the company of those who published it."*

Book design copyright © 2012 by Tate Publishing, LLC. All rights reserved.
*Cover and interior design by Stan Perl*
*Illustrations by Jason Hutton (based on original artwork by Lorraine Brodek)*

Published in the United States of America

ISBN: 978-1-62024-152-3
1. Juvenile Fiction / Holidays & Celebrations / Christmas & Advent
2. Juvenile Fiction / Social Issues / Bullying
12.06.13

# Dedication

To the most special grandson, Logan McLain Dunn,
for whom this book is written.

Always believe! Continue to be kind and to care
so Santa won't stuff your stocking with white
underwear. And as Peeky Peeper says: "May your
life be as bright as each Christmas tree light."

Cuddle up to read
(now that you're getting sleepy)
A Christmas-y tale
that's really rather peepy.

Santa sat at his messy desk in the North Pole. In front of him were papers and small bags of coal.

He unfolded a letter and scratched at his head.
Then he rechecked his *Good List* and thinkingly said,

"That Logan McLain has been a *goof-off* this year,
which means white underwear in his stocking, I fear.

I don't understand this, but maybe I should…
because he always writes me that he's been so good."

# *Good Letter:*

DEAR SANTA,

I HAVE BEEN VERY GOOD THIS YEAR. I WOULD LIKE A ROBOT AND LEGO'S.

GRANDMA AND I ARE ICING COOKIES FOR YOU.

LOVE, LOGAN McLAIN

"I think someone is framing poor Logan McLain and saying some naughty things about him again. We need to find out what the real answer is here, so I won't bring him those *Tighty Whities* this year."

# Naughty Letter:

Dear Santa,
   Logan McLain
has been bad
   this year. Please
bring him coal or
underpants.
   Signed,
      Anonymoose

"Look at the writing on this anonymous* note;
it's not the same as the one Logan just wrote."

*a-non-y-mous: 1) No name; 2) Writer unknownus.

"I shall summon Elf Carl to see what he thinks.
Because Logan McLain's being naughty just stinks."

So Santa buzzed Elf Carl, who hopped out of bed
and tripped over his toolbox and fell on Elf Fred.
"Oof, sorry, Elf Fred ... Santa needs us right away!
Come with me. We'll find out why and if he's okay."

With bells jingling on tips of their small pointy shoes,
they ran to Santa's office to find out the news.

"You two are quick," said Santa to elves Carl and Fred,
"Logan McLain's been naughty or so I've just read.
Something doesn't make sense and we must find out why.
Someone's writing bad things about our good little guy."

In a squeaky high voice, Elf Carl answered with glee,
"Peeky Peeper can help us. She lives in a tree!
She hides in the pine needles and sits on her light.
She can watch and hear everything all through the night.

She has teeny light buddies on her peeking team.
Peeky Peeper's pals are the answer to our scheme.
Nothing gets by them as they discover the truth.
They keep watch from four sides as they sneakily sleuth.
The Peep Team is tricky and can hang upside down,
and they don't get dizzy as they look all around.
Now let me introduce them since they're new in town."

# Team Peep

**Little Missy Toe**
… so Christmas-y and kissy.

**Green Tickle Pickle**
… all wrinkly and twinkly.

**Bubbly Rudy Float**
… so root beery and cheery.

**Chocolatey Cherri Sundae**
… creamy and dreamy.

**Shiny Penny Pencil**
… very yellow and bright.

**Licky Sticky Candi Cane** …
and **Little Boo White**.

Santa phoned Peeky Peeper and asked her to find
a person Logan might know who was not being kind.
Peeky Peeper was happy and let out a cheer,
which her team squeaked loudly into Santa Claus's ear.

## "CHEEP, CHEEP, CHEEP
## GO TEAM PEEP!

## PEEK, PEEK, PEEK
## WE NEVER SLEEP!"

They leaped to their tree lights and they watched and they peeked ...
and they hopped from light to light for almost one week.

Then one day Bully Bro pushed through Logan's front door and spied all the gifts under the tree on the floor.

He shoved Logan McLain and started being tough. Bully Bro yelled, "It's not fair to get so much stuff!" He poked and he threatened that again he would write about how bad Logan was to Santa … that night! This made Logan so sad, and he started to cry, and Bully Bro laughed since he knew it was a lie. "Just you see … Santa will skip you, Logan McLain. You'll just get underpants and not one candy cane!"

He heard Bully Bro laugh as he ran toward the street.
Logan saw him kick the fence with one of his feet.
Team Peep was all shocked as they witnessed this scene.
No doubt about it, bullies are bad and they're mean.
They ruin Christmas for all and don't spread the love.
They're rude and unkind and would much rather just
shove.

Logan thought for a moment on how to make this right.
"What can I do for Bully Bro so he won't fight?"
*I know,* he thought, *I'll take my best toy to his house.*
*I'll wrap it and leave it, then he won't be a louse!*
*Maybe being unhappy makes him so mean each year.*
*And maybe if I'm nice that will show him some cheer.*

This made Peeky Peeper cheep and leap on her light.
And all of Team Peep twinkled … oh what a bright sight!
She called Santa right then with a glowing review:
How Logan's naughty letter was surely not true
and that it was bad Bully Bro who needed the coal
and a letter from Santa from the North Pole.

But then Santa thought Bully Bro needed some care
and he should write a letter with love he could share.

Santa wants to turn every bad kid into good
so they do kind deeds all year as everyone should,
making our world better when we're young and small
so it's a great place to live when we're big and tall.

And that's Santa's message …

# Merry Christmas To All!

With love from Santa Claus, his elves, and Peeky Peeper's team,
who keep watch through the night with twinkling lights that gleam.

Peeky Peeper has a message too just for you
from all the Peeper members on her lighting crew:

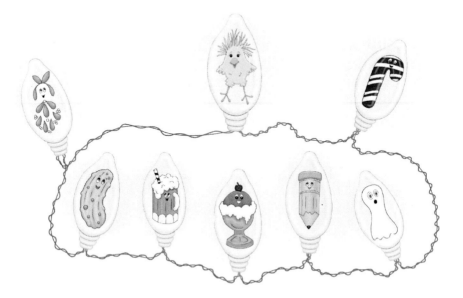

Team Peep will light up your Christmas tree every year
to make sure your holidays are filled with good cheer.
Please assign us a light on the very first night
to watch who's being good or not acting quite right.
Be sure to check the tree on the following days
and just watch how Team Peep has moved...

# you'll be amazed!

# May your year be as bright as each Christmas tree light!

# The Game of Peeky Peeper

(For grown-up eyes only):

Please have fun with your children cutting out each Team Peep member from the page. Then put sticky tape behind the paper* "Peepers" and press onto the base of your Christmas tree mini lights. Move the Peeper Players around from light to light after bedtime so that their position is constantly changing.

Catching good deeds and giving compliments is even more important than just "spying" and reprimanding for being naughty. Make the "Peepers" as easy or hard to find as you want! Your kids will love it!

**Disclaimer:** *These cutouts are for mini lights only and not to be placed on larger light bulbs that emit heat.*

Logan & Grandma LoLo

# listen|imagine|view|experience

## AUDIO BOOK DOWNLOAD INCLUDED WITH THIS BOOK!

In your hands you hold a complete digital entertainment package. In addition to the paper version, you receive a free download of the audio version of this book. Simply use the code listed below when visiting our website. Once downloaded to your computer, you can listen to the book through your computer's speakers, burn it to an audio CD or save the file to your portable music device (such as Apple's popular iPod) and listen on the go!

How to get your free audio book digital download:

1. Visit www.tatepublishing.com and click on the e|LIVE logo on the home page.
2. Enter the following coupon code:
   ce4a-184c-36a2-1b34-1f41-e4f1-646e-baa7
3. Download the audio book from your e|LIVE digital locker and begin enjoying your new digital entertainment package today!